JACK, THE KING OF ASHES

by Andy Jones
Illustrations by Darka Erdelji

JACK TALES
BY
ANDY JONES

For   Louis

Once upon a time, a long long time ago, in a tiny cove
on a little island off a big island off an even bigger island, there was
a widow lady who had three sons. Two were as good as gold –
Tom and Bill their names were; but the other fella was a lazy bag
o' bones! His name was Jack and all he ever did was sleep in the coal
box behind the stove. He never went to school; he never went to work.
There was *nothing* they could do with him. When he was fifteen years
old they say he finally got up outta the coal box, shook himself,
and a half-barrel of ashes fell off him.

"What are you doin outside the box?" says his mother.

"I was thinkin," he says, "thinkin I might go get a job."

"G'way, ya foolish gom," says his mother. "Who'd hire you,
ya useless article?" So Jack climbs back into the coal box.

"All I wanted was a bit of encouragement, Mudder," he says.

"I'll encourage ya," says his mother, shaking her fist.

Finally when Jack was twenty-one, his two brothers
up and declare they're going to leave home and search
for a lost princess – because whoever found her would
get her hand in marriage. At least that's what the king
said. (And I suppose if you can't trust the king who
can you trust?)

Now the mother was thinkin to herself: "I'm rid
of two 'em. How am I gonna get rid o' buddy
in the coal box?"

So one day she calls her brother Amberse over
and asks him what to do. "Get him a dog,"
says Amberse, "cause a dog is one thing
that'll always get you on the go."

And that did the trick. She gets Jack a little dog
and Jack names him Kevin-Phonse. Soon as ever
he gets the dog he jumps outta the coal box, shakes
himself, and a full barrel of ashes falls off him onto
the ground.

"By the jumpins," says Mother, "you, my son,
are the King of Ashes."

Jack likes that. "Yes, b'y," he says to himself, "I'm the King of Ashes and that's why I'm the one goin to marry that missing princess."

"After ya find her," says Kevin-Phonse.

Jack jumps back. "Did you say something?" he says to the dog.

But Kevin-Phonse just stands there, waggin his tail.

They say the dog could talk, but that he'd only say the odd thing, now and again. That might just be old foolishness.

Whatever way it was, Jack and Kevin-Phonse head off to find the king's daughter, the Princess Frederica. Her full name now, they say, was Frederica Marie Corella Van Vee Van Vettum. And that's some name.

Anyway, Jack and the dog, they dodge on down the road 'til they meet a robber on a long bridge.

"Give me all ya got!" says the robber.

"You already took it," says Jack.

"I took nothing," says the robber.

"And that's all I had.
So if you took nothing,
then ya musta took it from me."

JACK'S HOUSE

CAVE

X3

MORE TREAS

TWO SMALL BIRDS

6

The robber starts in to laugh. He says to Jack, "What're you doing now? Young fella like you, spose you're off tryin to find the missing princess."

"And that's what I'm not," says Jack. "That's one thing I'm not interested in, but I *am* lookin for a job."

Then the robber says to him, "Are ya any hand to rob?"

"Me, a robber?" says Jack.

"Yes," says the robber.

"Well," says Jack, "I spose I could learn."

"That's the spirit," says the robber. "You come wit me and my gang," he says, "and I'll show you the ropes. And yer dog'll come in handy too."

"Thank you kindly," says Kevin-Phonse.

"Did that dog just talk?" asks the robber.

"I don't think so," says Jack. "Never heard tell of a dog that could talk."

"Fair enough," says the robber.

Buddy takes him back to his cave and there's twelve beds all in a row.

And the fella says, "Yer first job is to make up them beds."
(This is the robbers' beds now, and there's twelve of 'em.)
"And I suppose you'll want yer own bed?"

"No," says Jack, "I always sleep in the coal box."

So that's how Jack and Kevin-Phonse become robbers.
Before you know it, they're the best robbers of 'em all.

Now, every day after a hard day's robbin, the whole gang meets on the long bridge and shows each other what they got. And without fail Jack and his dog always show up with the most. The robbers love 'em. They're the real high liners.

But one day
Jack gets home early and he doesn't
wait for the others, and he starts in to snoop
around the cave. After a while he sees Kevin-Phonse
sniffin and whimperin at a little door way
in the back. Then the dog starts to bark.
"Be quiet, ya fool," says Jack. But he jimmies
the door open and there's the Princess Frederica
herself, tied to a chair. Jack takes
the big bow and says,
"Ah, you must be
the princess."

"Yes," she says, "can ya help me?"

9

"Yes," he says, "shur, that's what I come for. I am Jack, the King of Ashes."

"Yes, b'y," says the princess, a bit skeptical.

But she soon realizes he is a good youngfella. He and Kevin-Phonse untie the princess, grab a big sack o' money from the robbers, and quick as a flash the three of 'em start to run out the door. They run like the mill-tails down the road 'til off in distance they see the robbers coming home a'wards the bridge.

"Oh my, we're caught!" says the princess. "What are we gonna do now?"

"Hide under the bridge," says Kevin-Phonse.

The princess says, "Did he just speak?"

"I don't think so," says Jack, "but I'm never sure."

Anyway they follow the dog's advice and under the bridge they go. They can hear one of robbers above sayin, "Where's Jack to?"

"Not like him to be late," says another.

"Don't suppose he's after runnin off," says another fella. "Maybe we better go back and check."

So back they go, and Jack and the princess up boot and give 'er down the road. They go so fast their feet hardly touch the ground. Then, off a little distance they see a cloud of dust coming down the road a'wards them.

"That's it," says Jack. "IT'S THE ROBBERS! We're done for."

Then they see this run-down old boarding house that hasn't seen a customer in years, with a sign out front reading *Hennessey's Boarding House, Mrs. Dorcas Hennessey, Proprietress.* Jack knocks on the door and says, "Missus Hennessey," he says, "there's some ruffians after us and they'll make away with us if they catches up. You got to hide us."

"Oh my," she says, "you go down in the cellar, I'll lift the hatch." Now there's a hatch under the coal box down to the basement. Then she says, "I got ta warn ya," she says, "there's a frightening sight down there."

"What's that?" says Jack, but before she can answer there's a brutal knock on the door.

"If Jack and they are in there, you let us in!" the robber says. "Let us in or we'll break yer windows and yer door!"

Too late. Mrs. Hennessey's front door comes crashing in and Jack and Frederica and Kevin-Phonse skedaddle down a rickety ladder and Mrs. Hennessey puts the coal box back over the hatch. She pretends she was haulin out a few scraps of coal for her old stove.

And Jack and them, frightened half to death, are crawlin around in the dark when Jack lights a candle and he looks at the princess and she's lookin over his shoulder and her eyes are as big as apples with fright. She had like to let out the biggest kinda howl, for there, down in the candlelight, she sees two corpses... two men, dead and laid out on the ground. She tries to climb back up the steps but she hears the robbers upstairs talkin to Mrs. Hennessey.

"Have you seen a man and a woman and a dog runnin for their lives nearby," says one of the bully-boys.

And she says, "Yes," she says, "I most certainly did see them."

Jack and the princess are frightened to death when they hear that. They think Mrs. Hennessey is gonna rat 'em out.

She says: "And I'll tell you just where they are! They are after runnin," she says, "right the way you're after coming from! How could you miss 'em?"

"I dunno, missus," he says, "but we'll get 'em this time."

"Yes, turn back, buddy! And you'll find 'em."

So the robbers run off in the wrong direction, and Jack and they come up from the cellar.
"Oh my," says Mrs. Hennessey to the princess, "I'm sorry, maid, you must have got some fright. But don't mind," she says "that's me husband and me son. They both died," she said, "in a accident in the mine. The tin mine. And I can't afford to bury 'em." Then she starts in to bawl her eyes out.

But the princess takes the old lady in her arms and comforts her. She says, "I know what you're feelin," she says. "Shur, me own mother died when I was only eight." Then Mrs. Hennessey starts comfortin the princess. Then the *two of 'em* are bawlin their eyes out.

Jack says, "Have you got either bit o' lumber here?"

"No," she says, "the only bit o' board here is in me kitchen table."
So Jack and the princess and Kevin-Phonse cut up the table
and make two coffins. Jack digs two deep holes and lays the two men
to rest with reverence and dignity.

Frederica makes up a little poem and says it over their graves:

"Who is to say why they goes away,
Who is to say where they goes –
But we loved 'em while they were here,
That's the only thing we knows."

Kickin his hind legs in the dirt Kevin-Phonse fills in
the grave holes. Jack makes a little sign sayin: *Hector and Darryl*
Hennessey – Rest In Peace.

Old Mrs H. is as delighted as she can be,
under the circumstances. Lot of people couldn't afford
to bury the dead in them days.

"My god, ye're that sweet," she says. "I could squeeze
the life outta the three o' ye."

And they all have a little giggle.

"And now," she says, "I got to give *you* something." And she goes and gets a lovely raglan coat with lovely silk lining all buttoned into it and gives it to Jack. "I want you to wear this raglan in memory of my son. It was his and it was the only good thing he ever had. He was just your age, buddy. Now, you three better high-tail it outta here; there's a ferryman can take you away from this little island to the big harbour on the big island. There, you'll find a ship to take you home."

As Jack is leavin he takes a little sack o' money from the big sack o' money and slips it to the old missus. A nice little sum, to tide her over and buy a proper headstone for her husband and son's graves. She's tickled pink.

Frederica and Jack and Kevin-Phonse start in to run like the devil at a Sunday-school picnic. They take the fast route on the high road to the ferry. And they soon find old Ted the ferryman sittin on the wharf and they tell him they got to get goin to the big island fast, that their lives are in danger.

"Eeeeeeeeee-yup ..." says Ted slowly, not budging from his chair. Nothing bothers Ted. He's the slowest fella on the island. He's only got two speeds – 'slow' and 'stop' – and precious little difference between them.

Ted starts fussin around with his ropes and his paddles 'til Jack is nearly out of his mind.

"Hurry," says Jack, "the robbers are comin over the hill!"

"Eeeeeeeeee-yup …" says Ted, slow as cold molasses.

"You're riskin our lives!" says the princess.

"This is ridiculous," growls Kevin-Phonse under his breath.

"Eeeeeeeeee-yup …" says Ted, as he *finally* pushes the boat into the water.

And sure enough they're just a hundred yards out into the tickle when the robbers get to the shore. They start shoutin for Ted to stop. They threaten him with every kind of bully-trick in the books. They even offer him money if he'll turn around; but Ted, by gar, he can't be shook. Once that ferryman started on a voyage nothing could make him turn back.

Soon they are at a port on the big island. Then, Ted turns around and is gonna head back to ferry *the robbers* across the water!!!

"No!" says Jack.

And guess what Ted says...

"Eeeeeeeeee-yup ..."

"No!" says Jack.

"Eeeeeeeeee-yup ..." says Ted.

"You mean you're gonna go back and get 'em even though they might make away with us."

"Eeeeeeeeee-yup," says Ted. "That's not my problem. I'm the ferryman. I ferry whoever wants to be ferried. I'll ferry 'til I'm buried. My father was a ferryman, his father was a ferryman and they ferried 'til they were buried.....so..."

Jack goes over and jumps a hole right through Ted's boat.

Well, Ted is fit to be tied. He is fumin! He's so mad he almost starts movin fast.

But Jack takes out another little sack o' money from the big sack o' money, gives it to Ted, and says, "This'll pay for your boat to be fixed and 'twill take care of you into your old age."

Ted's still mad, but at least he sees the good into it.

Then Jack, Frederica, and Kevin-Phonse come across a captain named Muldoon who agrees to carry them to Cumberland, the princess's homeland.

They get aboard the ship and everything is fine for a week or so. But that Captain Muldoon, he knows something's up. And finally one of his men tells him that the woman they got aboard is a famous missing princess with reward attached. Muldoon, well, he can't get it off his mind. He wants to be the hero and win the princess.

Now Jack and the king's daughter know nothing about this, and they are having a grand little trip. Every day they sit on the deck and read and tell stories and get to know each other.

But there's more to it than that – they start to fall in love. And I got to say they fall deeper and deeper and deeper in love as the time whittles away. And every day, while they're sittin on the deck, Frederica demands that Jack give her the raglan coat so she can 'do a little work on it'. Jack thinks the coat is fine as it is, but he doesn't want to argue. Then she works away with her sewing needle and at the end of each day she gives it back to Jack, but Jack can't see any difference in the coat.

"I don't know what in tarnation she's doin with the coat. Looks the same to me at the end of day as it does at the beginning," he thinks.

But he doesn't say anything cause sewing was one of the few things the princess's mother had time to teach her before she died. And that was a very special thing.

Then one evening, she goes off to bed and leaves her sewing basket on the deck and early the next morning Muldoon finds it. He sees his chance. He grabs the sewing basket and throws it overboard. Then he calls below for Jack, who's asleep in the coal box in the engine room, to go over the side and fetch the basket.

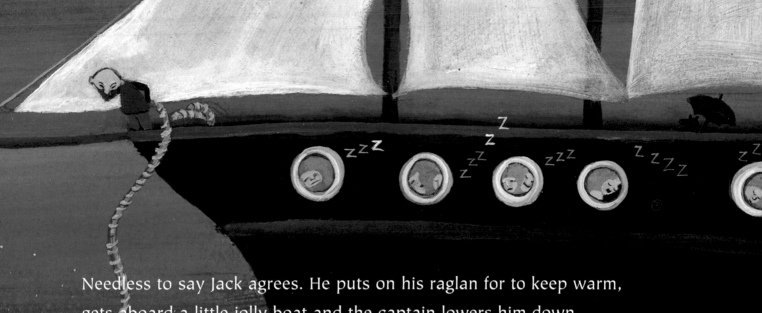

Needless to say Jack agrees. He puts on his raglan for to keep warm,
gets aboard a little jolly boat and the captain lowers him down.
Soon as ever Jack is on the water, Muldoon cuts the painter and leaves
Jack adrift on the water. Jack looks around and sees there's no paddles
aboard, and he knows he's finished.

Jack bawls out to the captain, "Hey, buddy, there's
no oars on this boat."

"Yes, b'y?" says Muldoon. "Oh my, things are tough
all over, wha?" Then he turns on his heel and disappears down below.
Jack sings out at the top of his lungs, but all hands are still asleep.

And soon Jack drifts outta sight of the ship.

Now the Princess Frederica is fast asleep in her cabin. She doesn't

The captain waits a few hours to report that Jack is missing.
The princess is inconsolable. She stands on the deck lookin
for Jack and cryin 'til she gives all her salt tears to the big sea.
And Kevin-Phonse stands at her side and matches her tear for tear.
He was what they call 'a one-man dog', and I spose she was
a one-Jack princess.

Jack meantime is driftin in his little boat. He looks around and says to himself. "That's it, b'ys. I'm finished. I'll try to just go to sleep and with any luck I'll wake up dead."

So he pulls his precious coat tight around him, lies down in the bow, and with a picture of the princess in his mind, he's soon fast asleep.

Then something wakes him up. It's a strange sound. Like rushing water. And then he realizes his boat is high in the air. He leans over the side and looks under it. And by gar, there's two ghosts holdin the boat up and movin 'er over the water as fast as can be. He calls out to the ghosts.

"Hang on there, b'ys. What are ye at?"

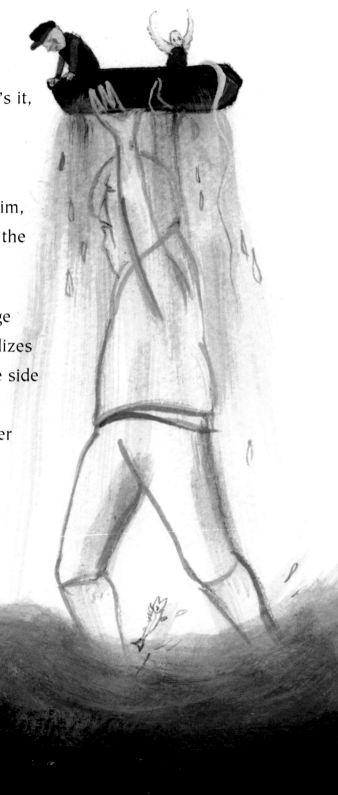

And quick as a wink the boat drops back to the ocean with the biggest
kinda sploosh, and what do you know but the two ghosts
are sittin in the stern of 'er lookin at Jack and
smiling scary lookin smiles.

They say, "Do you recognize us?"

"No," says Jack.

"Then look harder,"
say the ghosts.

Then it dawns on him.
"Oh my, Mrs. Hennessey's husband
and her son!"

"At your service," say the ghosts.

"Welcome aboard," says Jack. "I fancy this means my life is over."

"No, no, my son," says Mr. Hennessey. "You helped us to get coffins and a decent burial, so now we're gonna help you. Here's a rope," he says, "a Lapland rope. A magic rope. There's three knots into it. If you undo one knot the jolly boat will head in any direction ya want it to. Undo the second knot and it'll take you there as fast as can be. But don't," he says, "untie the third knot or it'll cause the worst kinda hurricane and you'll be drowned for sure."

"Fair enough," says Jack. "And I thank you. It'll take me to Cumberland and I can claim the princess's hand in marriage according to the king's decree."

Then the younger ghost, Darryl, says, "B'y," he says, "I can't explain this to you, bein as yer one of the living. But when you gets back on the land don't embrace or kiss anyone – man, woman, or beast – until the king gives his permission and you are engaged to the princess."

"Why?" says Jack. "What'll happen?"

"Well," says the ghost, "if you do so kiss or embrace, then the princess will forget you, forget that she ever met you, that you rescued her, that she fell in love with you, that you disappeared from the ship at sea. And though she might well fall in love with you anew, it will be too late, for she will be married to Muldoon."

"All right," says Jack. "I can do that, for luckily, the people of Cumberland are of Irish descent and not generally given to public displays of affection."

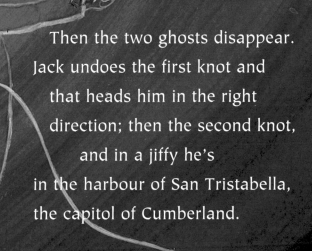

Then the two ghosts disappear.
Jack undoes the first knot and
that heads him in the right
direction; then the second knot,
and in a jiffy he's
in the harbour of San Tristabella,
the capitol of Cumberland.

And although he's right curious
about what'll happen
if he undoes the third knot,
he holds back.
Then he gets off the jolly boat and gets himself
a boarding house, careful not to do
any embracing or kissing.
Not that there's that much temptation.
But whatever way it was, he sits around waitin
for the princess to come home.

Couple days later Frederica and Kevin-Phonse and Captain Muldoon arrive at the government wharf in San Tristabella harbour.

The first thing the princess does is to tell her father all about Jack, how he rescued her and how he disappeared.

The king says, "Yes, girl," he says, "that's sad. He must have been some youngfella and I'm sure you loved 'en. But the man who brought you home is the man who will get your hand in marriage... and that'd be Captain Muldoon. My darling, it was a desperate time when you disappeared, you were gone for a long time and it called for a desperate measure. I'm sure you'll learn to love him as your mother did me; for as you know, our marriage, too, was arranged."

Then they share more than a few tears remembering the princess's mother, the dead queen, and the next day preparations begin for the wedding of Princess Frederica Marie Corella Van Vee Van Vettum and Captain Charles Olivier Cuthbert Muldoon.

Now, one day there is a crowd of young serving ladies laughin and whizgiggin about a handsome young man who had come ashore a few days before in a jolly boat with no oars and how he always wore a lovely coat with silk lining; and, though lots of girls and a few boys had tried, he would not allow anyone – woman, man, nor beast – to embrace or kiss him. 'Twas the talk of the harbour. This makes the princess very curious and early one morning she locks Kevin-Phonse in her room and sets out to see if she can at least clap eyes on buddy.

Kevin-Phonse, now, is none too happy to be barred in the castle and he starts in to scheme how to get out and follow her.

It doesn't take Frederica long to find Jack. He's sittin in a chair outside his boarding house.

Their eyes meet, and their hearts near explode with joy. Then all of a sudden, Jack turns tail, runs, and climbs a tree. "Oh my," the princess thinks, "he's off hees trolley."

But no, Jack explains it all from the tree, how the captain put him overboard, how the grateful dead men helped him, how he can embrace or kiss neither man nor woman nor beast 'til they are engaged to be married.

The princess falls on her knees and laughs with joy. "Come down," she says, "and return with me to me father. I will tell him the rights of everything."

Jack climbs down the tree. He and Frederica are happier
than ever they'd been, knowing at last they would live
lives in love. And she says, "Now, Jack," she says,
"I got to tell you something important about your coat.
When I tell my father the truth, Muldoon is gonna argue.
But that coat will prove…"

But before she can finish, Kevin-Phonse comes running
down the hill. He's got away from the princess's room,
sniffed her down, and made the big tracks straight to Jack.
Jack is delighted, and just as he puts his arms around
the dog and the dog licks him and kisses him as only
a heartbroken dog can, he hears the princess cry out, "No!!"

Then Jack looks up. Something has changed in Frederica's eyes.

"Oh, sir," she says politely, "your dog truly loves you.
What's his name?"

Tiny cracks begin to appear in Jack's heart.

"Don't you know?"

"No, sir," she says. "How would I? Shur, I've never
seen him before."

Jack is in bits as he quietly murmurs:
"His name is Kevin-Phonse. He's a good dog.
Goodnight, Madame."

She says, "Goodnight, sir, nice meeting your dog … and you."
She stops, turns back to Jack, and she says: "You seem sad."

Holding back sobs, he says: "Freddie, don't you know me?"

She looks him hard up and down and says, "You do look familiar,
but I don't recall where I met you. I must get home now for my dad
will be looking for me. I am to be married in three days, though
it breaks my heart. Farewell, sir."

And that's it. The end.

This story, my friends, is over…

Or it should be.
But as you know, our Jack is not one to give up.

He stays up the whole night long walkin the streets
of San Tristabella with his faithful dog, having a big think
on how he's going to get through to Princess Frederica's

Now at this time in Cumberland, with a royal wedding in the works, there are actors and musicians and dancers and circus troupes showing up in the kingdom from all over the world, and since the princess is famous for her love of puppets, San Tristabella is suddenly lousy with puppeteers and their marionettes, with shadow shows, finger puppets, Vietnamese water puppets, bunrakus, sock puppets, glove puppets, Punch and Judys, tickle-bugs, and ventriloquists' dummies.

Jack is on a street corner watching a shadow show when he gets an idea! He says to himself:

"A puppet show! That'll be the perfect stroke
To give the conscience of that girl a poke."

hand puppet
(mimic puppet)

Kevin–Phonse rolls his eyes.

So now of course he has to get a puppet show together and to hire someone to make the puppets. So he goes to Delilah Daley, Cumberland's finest puppet-maker.

Some say Delilah had the face of a witch and others that she was the most beautiful woman in the world. In any event she always kept her face hidden by a veil for they say if anyone is not truly in love with their spouse and they look into Delilah's eyes, they will fall in love with her and pine for her 'til they die.

Jack doesn't care about that. Up he goes and knocks on her door.

"Come in," she says. "Now, listen," she says, "I keep my face masked because…"

"Yes, yes, I know," says Jack. "I heard the story. But I'm sure of my love, so I got no problem lookin you square in the face." So she takes off her veil and, at first, her face frightens Jack, but soon he begins to see its beauty, and although he doesn't fall in love with her, he can see how some might.

Anyhow he tells Delilah the story that he wants told in the puppet show and she agrees to make the puppets.

So on the day before the wedding Jack dresses up as a traveller and he dresses Kevin-Phonse up as an old lady, and he goes up and offers to perform his puppet play before the royal court. The princess is thrilled. And so Jack begins his show. It's called *Queen Aphrodite's Chicken*. And, b'ys, I got to say it was some good show.

But it's meant now to do a job on the princess, you know, to thaw out her memory.

So Jack begins to tell the story and move the puppets around.

Kevin-Phonse dressed as the old woman plays the guitar.

"Once upon a time," says Jack, "Queen Aphrodite had a pet chicken named Helen and she loved it. She fed that chicken and stroked that chicken 'til that chicken was fat and fluffy and spoiled rotten.

"Now there was a French chef in the palace kitchens and he was dyin to cook up that chicken for the king's supper:

> *Oh chicken, plump and juicy! Oh biddy, so sublime,*
> *I'll chop you up; you'll feed the king as soon as you are mine.*

"He knew the king would reward him if he served up that chicken. So one night he and a gang of evil sous-chefs sneak into Queen Aphrodite's chambers and steal the pudgy little Helen. The next day the queen is heartbroken that her little beauty is gone. The whole palace is in a tizzy. But she isn't the only one who is sad. There was a poor young rooster named Bogstar, who lived in the swamp at the bottom of the queen's kitchen garden where they threw the ashes from the palace stoves. Bogstar loved that glamorous little chicken. Many a night he sang outside her window:

> *Helen, oh Helen, oh beauteous chicken,*
> *When you turns me away, my heart takes a lickin.*
> *Oh Helen, I'd say,*
> *You're the best in the bay!*
> *The most wondrous sight*
> *In all of the bight!*
> *The cream of the cove,*
> *You near got me drove!*
> *And though they all say that you can be quite fickle –*
> *I know that I'd die for just one tiny tickle.*

shadow puppet

45

KITCHEN

"So, when the young rooster overhears
the boo-hooin and the hulaballooin and
the story of the capture of the beauteous Helen
by the Parisian chef, he waits 'til the next
morning and sneaks into the royal kitchens
and leaves tickets to the horse races.

"You see, the chefs and sous-chefs love the
horses, and so they quickly abandon the kitchens
and head to the race track.

"As soon as they are gone, Bogstar the rooster
bravely goes back into the kitchen opens the tiny
door to a little cave in the wall, and carries the
precious little treasure home to Queen Aphrodite.

"But do you think that chubby chicken is thankful?
No, my friends, she ignores the brave rooster
and when he begs her to speak to him she laughs
cruelly, 'I am Aphrodite's chicken. Why should
I remember a common rooster from the ashes
at the bottom of the kitchen garden?'

marionette
(sicilian)

For forty nights he tried to win her,
Told her how she'd nearly been dinner.
She scoffed and told him to depart.

This rooster died of a broken heart!

When Helen saw his broken body,
She knew her conduct had been shoddy.
There was no one else to blame –

Then Chicken Helen died of shame!"

Java style puppet

Princess Frederica is weeping at the end of the story, and Jack, still dressed as the troubadour, says to her, "Missus, are you cryin?"

"Oh, puppet man, why do you tell such a sad story?"

"Why do you find it so sad?" says Jack. "Does it remind you of your own deeds?"

"Yes," she said. "I have suddenly remembered something that happened to me. I must leave you, troubadour. I have an important errand." She throws on her cloak and starts to run off, when Jack pulls off his disguise and says, "Where are you going, my love?"

She looks at Jack and her eyes grow bigger and bigger, bigger even than the day she saw the dead Hennesseys. But no words will come. She runs to him and is just about to throw her arms around him when Kevin-Phonse, still disguised as the old lady and growling crazily, throws off his guitar, jumps up, grabs the back of her dress, and pulls her away from Jack.

"Kevin-Phonse get down!" Jack shouts. "Ya bad dog."

"No, no," said Frederica, "he's keeping us from embracing – in case we rekindle the spell. We must tell my father and the world of our love but we must not kiss … until we are sworn to each other. I will stop the marriage to Muldoon right now. Go get me your silk-lined raglan."

Now when she tells the rights of it to the king and the parliament of Cumberland, needless to say Muldoon kicks up the biggest kinda stink. He says: "I fulfilled the letter of the king's decree, and furthermore, I can't remember Jack bein on my ship at all."

Then the princess says to him, "Well, b'y," she says, "do you remember me sewin a silk-lined coat every day?"

"Yes," he says, "I remember that."

Then she calls Jack in. He's wearin the coat.

"Is this the coat?" she says to Muldoon. "Yes, my sweet," he says, "that's the coat, but it doesn't prove anything."

"That's the very coat," she says, "that everyone seen this man wearin when he stepped off the oarless jolly boat. And the truth is in that coat!! Jack, come forward and read what's written inside the coat!"

Jack looks inside, but he can't see anything. "Sorry, my darling, but there's nothing written there."

Jack
the King of Ashes

"Unbutton the lining, ya fool," she says. And when he does it's plain to see the whole true story is sewn into the coat: how Jack saved her from the robbers, how they ran away, how they buried the Hennessey men, met Ted the ferryman, got aboard Muldoon's ship, how they fell head over heels in love, and how they thought Muldoon was jealous...

"That's what you were up to with yer needle," says Jack.

"Yes, my love, my dove, my duckie!" she says.

Well, that's good enough for king and parliament. Muldoon is thrown
in jail and the king announces that Jack and Frederica will tie the knot.
Soon as the words are out of his mouth
there are safe hugs all round,
and the two young lovyers exchange
a kiss that was said to be the
greatest kiss since kissing began –
at least that was *their* claim and
no one argued.

Jack insists that the wedding be held on Hallowe'en night so that
the dead Hennesseys can attend. And they come with bells on.
As do the beloved dead queen mother and even Kevin-Phonse's
deceased doggie-parents.

It's a grand affair – a wedding *and*
a Hallowe'en party – held in a circus tent,
and among the living attendees are
Dorcas Hennessey herself, Ted the ferryman
(who arrived late), and Jack's brothers Tom and Bill. And 'Mudder'.

And to everyone's astonishment, just before midnight the ghost of Jack's father appears, and he pulls Jack and the princess aside, and he says,

"Jack, b'y, I only got a few minutes to tell you why you've stayed in the coal box all these years. Y'see, when you were a wee lad of four years I told you I'd start the next day to teach you some carpentry skills, and that our first job would be to build a new coal box. But the very next day I drowned. I suppose you must have gone to the coal box and waited for me to return. And you never left. So now that you know, perhaps you can start sleeping in a real bed."

"Yes," says Jack.

"Thank goodness," says the princess.

Jack's mother is the hit of the party and she toasts the king's family
with a little poem:

What happens to youngsters is wonderful queer –
They drive you so nuts you go on the beer.
Then all of a sudden they shake off their ashes,
And you wonder what caused your weeps and your gnashes.

I gave up on young Jack, I got to admit;
I begged and I pleaded but he wouldn't submit.
When I heard he ran off with a gang of sleveens,
I thought, well, that's it – it must be in his genes.

Then he met that sweet princess and never looked back.
Can love be a cure for all what we lack?
I think it must be, and Jack proves it true;
And Frederica confirms it, for she's happy too.

So whenever you think to yourself, "It's a bust!"
A positive outlook is really a must.
Shur, I thought me n' Jack would end up in the gutter
But, by gar, there's a princess now callin me 'mudder'!

And as they are about to leave the table, Kevin-Phonse stands up, raises a glass of champagne and says, "Come ahead with good luck the rest of our lives!"

Everyone stops.

"Did that dog just speak?" says the king.

"No, ya foolish gom," says Mudder. "Shur, dogs can't talk."

Jack, the King of Ashes is, in part, a retelling of two Newfoundland folk tales: "The King of Ashes' Daughter", as told by Ambrose Reardon of Croque, White Bay; and "Jack and the Princess", as told by William B. Hewitt of Barr'd Islands, Notre Dame Bay. It also retells an incident in "The Green Man of Eggum", as told by Freeman Bennett of St. Paul's. These tellings were recorded and published in Herbert Halpert and John Widdowson's seminal collection *Folktales of Newfoundland*. These stories are themselves re-tellings of many tales, including the old ballad "The Factor's Garland".

Jack, the King of Ashes takes inspiration for the character Ted from Marriott Edgar's poem "The Runcorn Ferry", and for the last line ("dogs can't talk") from the poem "Evings's Dorg 'Orspital" by Charles Pond. The princess is based on Andy Jones's maternal grandmother Frederica (Winsor) Dobbin who always claimed her real name was Frederica Marie Corella Van Vee Van Vettum. The puppet-maker was inspired by Darka Erdelji. Kevin-Phonse is based on ghost dogs Bert, Maggie, Caper, Buddy, and Fogo, as well as living dogs Luna, Cooper, and Trouty.

Andy Jones would like to thank Mary-Lynn Bernard, and Marthe and Louis for their encouragement and support, as well as the City of St. John's Arts Jury for their financial contribution to the writing process. Mark Ferguson, Susan Williams, Betty-Jo Moore, Petrina Bromley, Christine Brubaker, Chantal Rancourt, Roy Logan, Camille Fouillard, Mary Win Clair, Don McKay, Alice Ferguson-O'Brien, Monique Tobin, Robert Joy, Veselina Tomova, Tara Bryan, and Maisie Rillie all read or listened to early drafts of this piece and made great suggestions. Andy especially wants to thank editor Marnie Parsons, and the North Star for all Newfoundland storytellers, Anita Best.

Darka would like to thank Andy Jones and Marnie Parsons for their trust and patience, and her family for their support.

An acclaimed actor, writer, and storyteller, Andy Jones is from St. John's, Newfoundland. He has had a long career in theatre, television, and film. Andy is a contributing author to *The Plays of Codco* and *Three Servings*, and is the author and narrator of the audio book *Letters from Uncle Val*. With Philip Dinn, he adapted the Newfoundland folktale *Peg Bearskin*, illustrated by Elly Cohen. His on-going series of Jack tales has been widely celebrated: *The Queen of Paradise's Garden* was named to the International Youth Library's White Ravens List, and shortlisted for both the NL History and Heritage Award and the Bruneau Family Award for Children's/Young Adult Literature – one of the Newfoundland and Labrador book awards; *Jack and the Manger* was shortlisted for the NL History and Heritage award, and received the 2012 Bruneau Family Award; *Jack and Mary in the Land of Thieves* received both the 2014 Bruneau Family Award and the 2012 BMO Winterset Award (only the second time in the award's history that a children's book has been so honoured).

A native of Slovenia, Darka Erdelji received a Masters of Arts in Puppet Scenography from Prague's Akadmie Muzickych Umeni. She lived in St. John's with her Newfoundland-born partner and their children for several years; during that time, she began collaborating with Andy Jones, first on the puppet play "The Queen of Paradise's Garden", and then on their acclaimed series of illustrated Jack tales. Darka currently designs puppets for Lutkovno Gledališče Maribor, a state-of-the-art Slovenian puppet theatre housed in a renovated medieval monastery.

The typeface is Tiepolo; it was created at AlphaOmega Typography
for the International Typeface Corporation in 1987.
Designed by Veselina Tomova of Vis-à-Vis Graphics,
St. John's, Newfoundland and Labrador.
Printed by The Lowe-Martin Group, Ottawa, Ontario.

ISBN 978-1-927917-01-5 (trade paperback)
ISBN 978-1-927917-02-2 (hardcover)

Running the Goat
Books & Broadsides
Cove Road
Tors Cove, Newfoundland and Labrador
A0A 4A0
www.runningthegoat.com